S0-AZO-936

BAA! MOO!
WHAT WILL WE DO?

For Doris and George
~A.H.B.

For Matthew and Sally
~J.C.

tiger tales
5 River Road, Suite 128, Wilton, CT 06897
This edition published in the United States 2020
Originally published in the United States 1996 as *What If?* by Little Tiger Press Ltd.
First paperback edition (978-1-58925-381-7) published in the United States 2003
Originally published in Great Britain 1996
by Little Tiger Press Ltd.
Text copyright © 1996 A.H. Benjamin
Illustrations copyright © 1996 Jane Chapman
Visit Jane Chapman at www.ChapmanandWarnes.com
ISBN-13: 978-1-68010-195-9
ISBN-10: 1-68010-195-1
Printed in China
LTP/1400/2971/0919
10 9 8 7 6 5 4 3 2 1

For more insight and activities, visit us at www.tigertalesbooks.com

BAA! MOO!
WHAT WILL WE DO?

BY
A. H. BENJAMIN

ILLUSTRATED BY
JANE CHAPMAN

tiger tales

Something special was about to happen at Buttercup Farm. The farmer had brought a kangaroo back with him from Australia. She was going to arrive that day!

All the animals gathered in the barnyard to talk about it. No one had ever seen a kangaroo before.

"What can a kangaroo do, anyway?" everyone wanted to know.

"What if she can crow?" asked Rooster. "What if she gets up very early and crows very loudly, and wakes up the whole farm? And what if she counts the chickens and hens to see if any are missing? If she does all that, the farmer won't need me anymore. I'll have to look for a new job!

Cock-a-doodle-doo!

What if I can't find another job?"

"How terrible!"

everyone said.

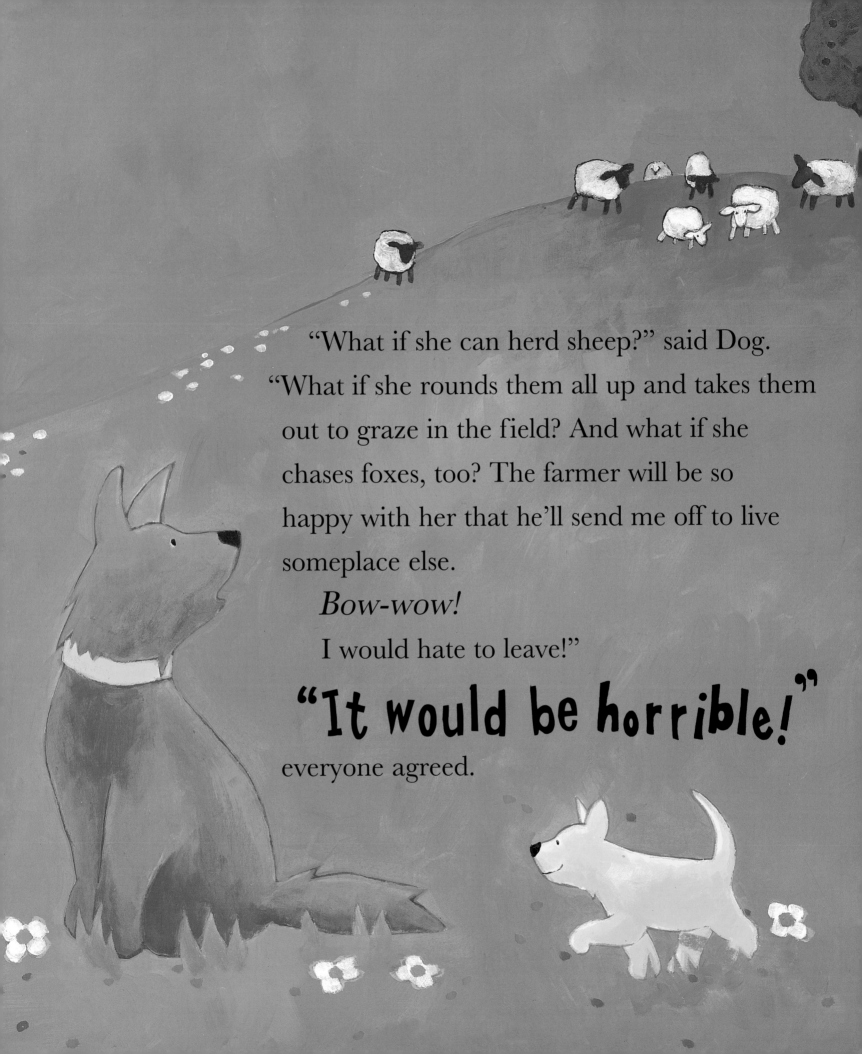

"What if she can herd sheep?" said Dog. "What if she rounds them all up and takes them out to graze in the field? And what if she chases foxes, too? The farmer will be so happy with her that he'll send me off to live someplace else.

Bow-wow!

I would hate to leave!"

"It would be horrible!"

everyone agreed.

"What if she can catch mice?" said Cat.
"What if she catches all the mice in the barn,
and the rats, too? And what if even the spiders
are afraid of her? Then the farmer wouldn't
need me anymore, and I would become a
stray cat looking for food in the trash!
Meow!
I would miss my fresh milk!"

"How awful!

said everyone.

"What if she can give milk?" asked Cow. "What if she fills up all the buckets in the barn with such creamy milk that people will rush to buy it? Then nobody would want my milk, and I'd have to pull the heavy plow through the field instead.

Moo!

I couldn't stand that!"

"How shocking!"

everyone said.

"What if she grows wool?" asked Sheep. "What if she has a thick, woolly fleece, softer and whiter than mine? And what if her wool grows twice as fast as mine does? The farmer would be so happy with her that he'd only use my wool for rags instead of nice sweaters.

Baa!

I don't want my wool used for rags!"

"How terrible!"
everyone agreed.

"What if she can pull a cart?" asked Horse. "What if she takes a cartful of fruit and vegetables to the market faster than I do? And what if she gives rides to the farmer's children? There would be no place here for me then, and I'd end up in the stable with all the old horses!

Neigh!

I'm too young to live in that old stable!"

"**How frightful!**"

said everyone.

The animals were getting worried. They were
so busy worrying that they didn't notice that some
of the younger animals had wandered away.

"Where are my puppies?" asked Dog.

"And my kittens?" asked Cat.
Sheep couldn't find her lamb, either.

The animals searched all over
the farm, but not a kitten, puppy,
or lamb was in sight.
They looked from the barn . . .

. . . to the pigsty, with no luck.

"This is horrible!" crowed Rooster.

"Terrible!" woofed Dog.

"Awful!" meowed Cat.

"Shocking!" mooed Cow.

"Frightening!" baaed Sheep.

"This is very bad!" neighed Horse.

    Suddenly, across the field they saw . . .

... a very strange animal, leaping and jumping toward them.

"Hello!" she said.
"I'm Kangaroo!"

The animals stopped searching
for their children. They stared at
Kangaroo. This new animal had
a large pouch on her stomach,
and in the pouch . . .

. . . were
three kittens,
two puppies,
and one lamb!

"I found your babies," said Kangaroo. "I'm a babysitter. I take care of the children and give them a ride in my pouch when they get tired. They love it!"

"What a great idea!" the animals cried. And crowing and barking and meowing and mooing and baaing and neighing, they all welcomed Kangaroo to Buttercup Farm.

A.H. BENJAMIN

A.H. Benjamin was born in Algeria, where he studied
physics and chemistry. He has written children's books
since 1987 and has had several books published by
Little Tiger Press. He is married with four children
and now lives in Lincolnshire, England.

JANE CHAPMAN

Jane has been illustrating for more than twenty years and
has produced many best-selling and award-winning titles.
She lives in Dorset, England, with her husband,
illustrator Tim Warnes. They have two sons.